D0122878

Eloise's Summer Vacation

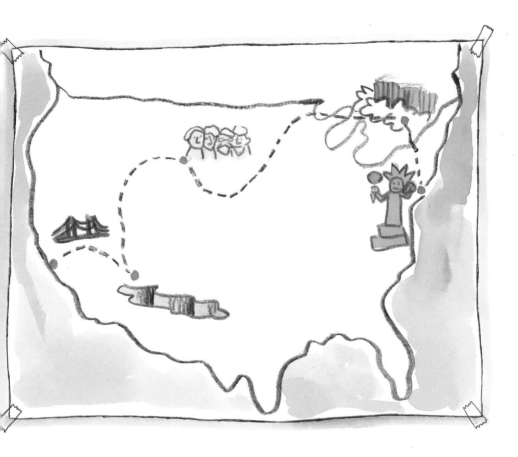

KAY THOMPSON'S ELOISE

Eloise's Summer Vacation

WITHDRAWN

STORY BY **Lisa McClatchy**

ILLUSTRATED BY **Tammie Lyon**

Ready-to-Read

Aladdin

NEW YORK · LONDON · TORONTO · SYDNEY

ALADDIN PAPERBACKS
An imprint of Simon & Schuster Children's Publishing Division
1230 Avenue of the Americas, New York, NY 10020
Copyright © 2007 by the Estate of Kay Thompson
All rights reserved, including the right of reproduction
in whole or in part in any form.
"Eloise" and related marks are trademarks of the Estate of Kay Thompson.
READY-TO-READ is a registered trademark of Simon & Schuster, Inc.
ALADDIN PAPERBACKS and related logo are registered trademarks of
Simon & Schuster, Inc.
The text of this book was set in Century Old Style.
Manufactured in the United States of America
First Aladdin Paperbacks edition May 2007
8 10 9 7
Library of Congress Control Number 2006933268
ISBN-13: 978-0-689-87454-3
ISBN-10: 0-689-87454-5
0511 LAK

"Eloise,"
   Nanny says,
"it is time to pack!"

Nanny and I
are going on vacation.
I know just what to bring!

This is the Butler.
He is also the driver.

Nanny sits up front.
She has her own TV.

Weenie and I try to sit.
Sometimes we do.

Sometimes we don't.
"Stay in your seats!"
Nanny says.

"First stop!"
says the Butler.

"Niagara Falls!" I say.

Weenie and I
like the spray.

We get very wet.
Oh I love Niagara Falls!

Being on the road is fun.
I brush Nanny's hair.

I brush Weenie's hair.

I try to brush
the Butler's hair.
"No, no, no!" says Nanny.

"Next stop!"
says the Butler.
"Mount Rushmore!"
I say.

I take my art supplies.
Nanny and the Butler pose.

Nanny looks like Lincoln.
So does the Butler.
Oh I love Mount Rushmore.

"Third stop!"
says the Butler.

"The Grand Canyon!"
I say.

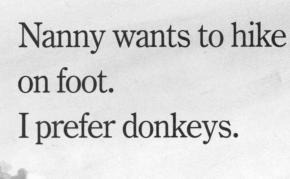

Nanny wants to hike
on foot.
I prefer donkeys.

So does Weenie.
The Butler prefers
to nap.

We win.
We ride to the bottom.
Oh I love the Grand Canyon!

"Last stop!"
says the Butler.
"San Francisco!"
I say.

"To the hotel!" says Nanny.
"To the hotel!"
   says the Butler.

"Do they have
room service?" I say.

Oh I love,
love, love vacation!